Lois G. Grambling

Daddy Will Be There

Pictures by
Walter Gaffney-Kessell

Greenwillow Books, New York

For four loving fathers:
my father, my father-in-law,
my husband, and my son
—L. G. G.

For my father
—W. G.-K.

A combination of airbrushing and watercolors was used for the full-color art.
The text type is Korinna.
Text copyright © 1998 by Lois G. Grambling
Illustrations copyright © 1998 by Walter Gaffney-Kessell
http://www.williammorrow.com
Printed in Hong Kong by South China Printing Company (1988) Ltd.
First Edition 10 9 8 7 6 5 4 3 2 1

Library of Congress Cataloging-in-Publication Data
Grambling, Lois G.
Daddy will be there / by Lois G. Grambling ;
pictures by Walter Gaffney-Kessell.
p.   cm.
Summary: Describes what a young girl does each day,
confident because she knows her father is there if she needs him.
ISBN 0-688-14983-9
[1. Fathers and daughters—Fiction.   2. Self-confidence—Fiction.]
I. Gaffney-Kessell, Walter, ill.   II. Title.
PZ7.G7655Dad   1998   [E]—dc20
96-5807   CIP   AC

play alone in my room.
I build with my blocks.

I read my picture books.
I hug my rag doll.

I look down the hall into the kitchen . . .
I know Daddy will be there.

I play alone in my backyard.
  I pull my red wagon.
I give my teddy bear a ride.
I give my stuffed alligator a ride.

I look up at the window . . .
I know Daddy will be there.

I ride my bike on the front walk.

My bike's wheel hits a rock.
My bike topples over.

My knee needs fixing.

I limp up the steps to my house . . .
I know Daddy will be there.

 run in the field next to my house.

I hide behind a blueberry bush.
I watch yellow butterflies
and fluffy white clouds.

I watch a ladybug
crawl across my foot.
I watch a cricket watching me.

I stand up and look across the field
to my house . . .
I know Daddy will be there.

 visit Emily at her house.

We play in her basement.

We play with her dolls and her dollhouse.

We play with her dinosaurs.

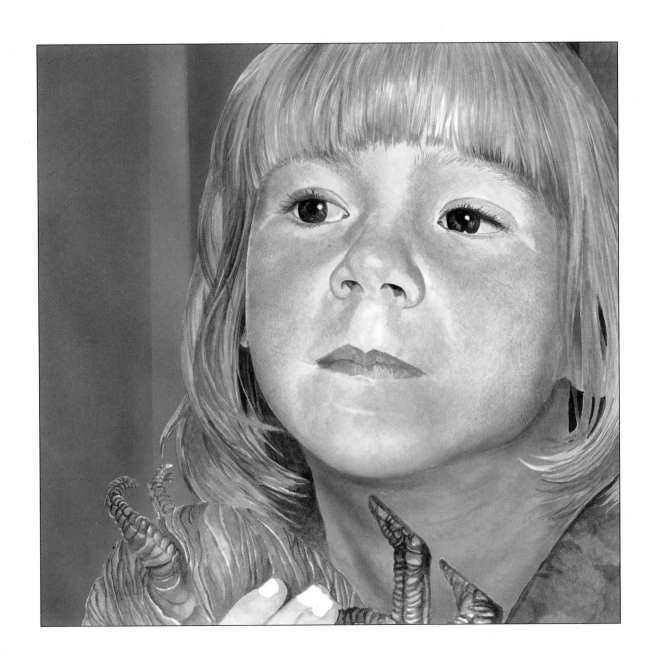

I stop playing and listen.
I hear voices upstairs.
I hear coffee cups clinking . . .
I know Daddy will be there.

I go to Christopher's birthday party.
We play "Pin the Tail on the Donkey."
We sing "Happy Birthday."
We eat birthday cake and
strawberry ice cream.

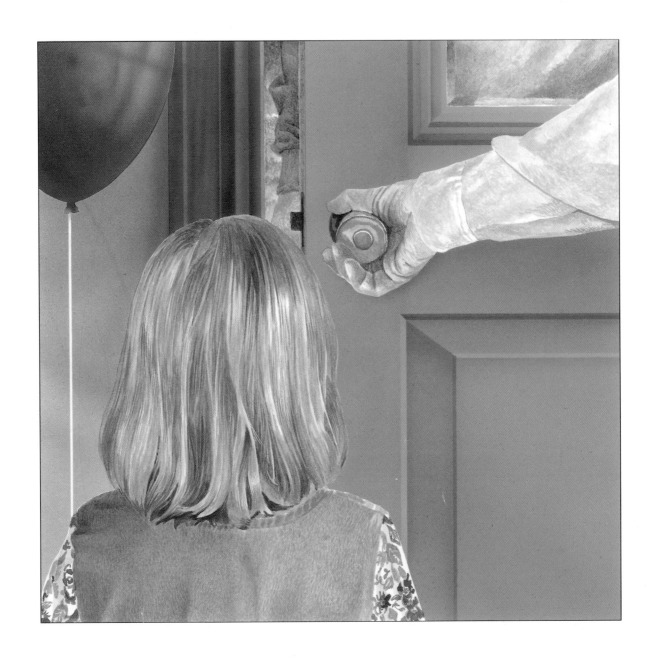

The presents are all unwrapped.
The party is over.
A red balloon is tied to my wrist.
The doorbell rings . . .
I know Daddy will be there.

go to kindergarten!
Daddy walks me to the door.
I walk in by myself.

I meet new friends.
We paint and share milk and cookies
and draw our families
with pointy new crayons.

When my teacher says, "Time to go home,"
I get my sweater from my cubby.
I unclip my painting from the clothesline.

I know Daddy will be there.

I walk out the door.
I climb into the yellow school bus.
The bus will take me to my house . . .